Under My Sombrero

by Anne E. Schraff
illustrated by Deborah Zemke

Richard C. Owen Publishers, Inc.
Katonah, New York

Under my sombrero flew a bat.

She was followed by a mouse and then a cat.

All of them squeezed under my sombrero.

Under my sombrero leaped a frog.

He was followed by a pig and then a dog.

All of them squeezed under my sombrero.

A sombrero is a great big hat.
But it's not big enough
for all of that.

Now there's no one here but me, under my sombrero.

DO
NOT
GO
AROUND
THE
EDGES

POEMS BY
DAISY UTEMORRAH

ILLUSTRATED BY
PAT TORRES

Magabala Books

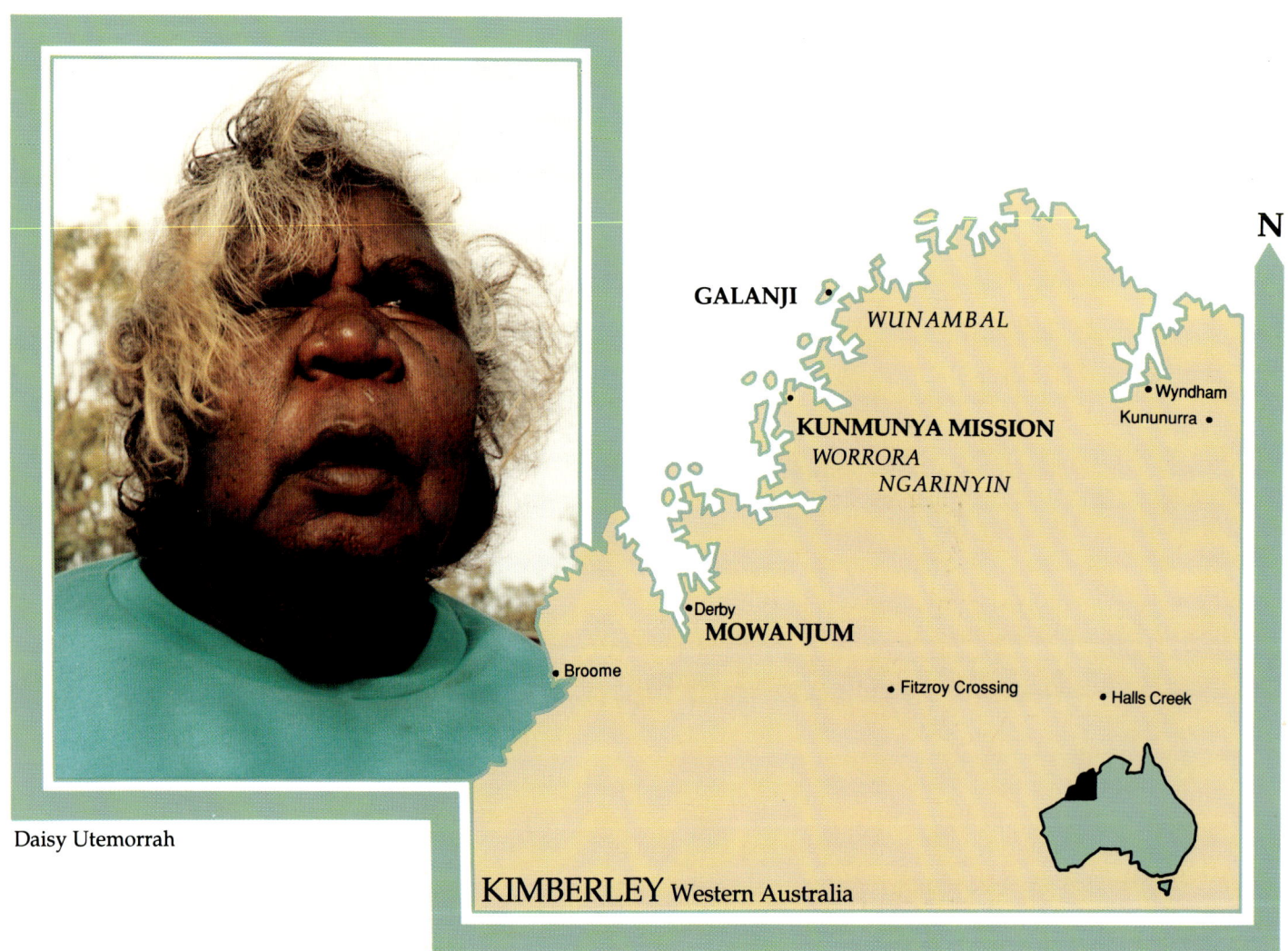

Daisy Utemorrah

KIMBERLEY Western Australia

Scale: 15mm : 100km

CONTENTS

Story About My Life   1 - 29

DO NOT GO AROUND THE EDGES   1
GALINJI   3
WATTLE TREE   5
BURUN BURUN THE KINGFISHER   7
RAIN   9
BIND WITH THE WHITE MAN'S LAW   11
A CRICKET   13
MOTHER'S TOUCH   15
WANDJINAS   16
WILLY WAGTAIL ABOUT THE TRIBAL WAR   19
POET   21
CAT   23
A DOG'S TALE   25
BLACK MAN   27
OUR MOTHER LAND   29

Story About My Life

DO NOT GO AROUND THE EDGES

Do not go around the edges
or else you'll fall.
No good that place
or else you slip.

I was born in Kunmunya Mission in February 1922. From my childhood I lived with my parents, in a humpy.

The mission didn't have many houses in those days, and so the people lived in huts. Years and days went on.

GALANJI

Far far away far far away
is my Island home
called Galanji
Far far away!
Far far away
is my Island home!
Aw-aw-aw.

As I was growing I went to church. I still lived in the camp. When I was five I went to school; I had to face it.

I thought I was leaving my parents but when I found I still went back to the camp I was happy. We only had school in the mornings.

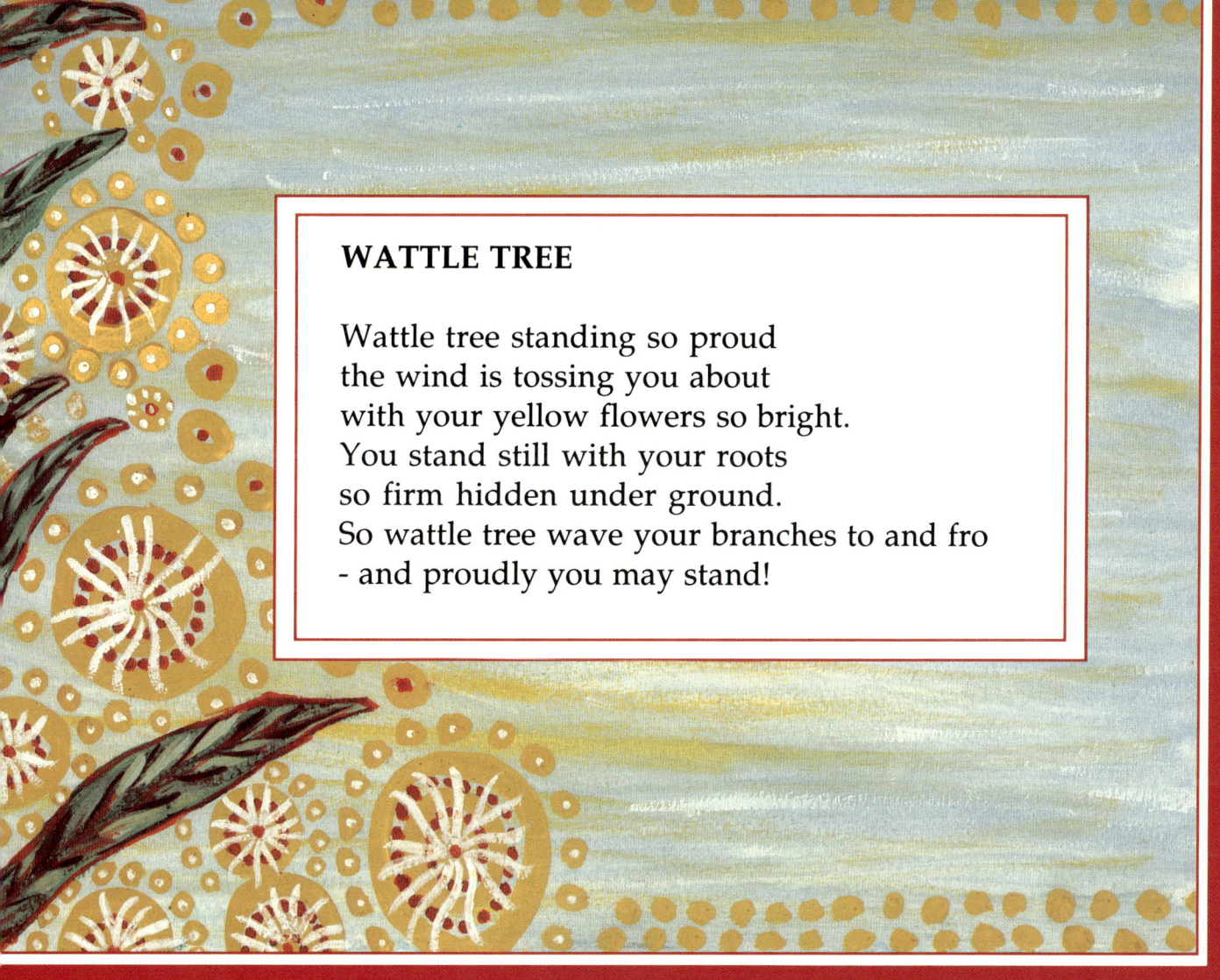

WATTLE TREE

Wattle tree standing so proud
the wind is tossing you about
with your yellow flowers so bright.
You stand still with your roots
so firm hidden under ground.
So wattle tree wave your branches to and fro
- and proudly you may stand!

In the afternoons we worked in the gardens, weeding or picking fruits or helping the women to water. That wasn't easy. We had to walk down with the buckets and get the water from the river.

On Saturdays I went bush walkabout for wild honey and bandicoots. We took dogs as well. That's the only day we went out. Not Sunday; we kept it holy.

BURUN BURUN THE KINGFISHER

"I am the kingfisher, Burun Burun they call me.
On a bright and sunny day I took my dog
named Ganganaw Lornya.
As I climbed on the hills
she found a kangaroo and chased it!
And she was so long
I started to call out, bair-bair
Ganganaw Lornya!

"Still she was missing
the more I called out, bair-bair...
At last she returned and came running up -
I was so angry I hit her across the nose
and she fell to the ground.

"That was the end of her,
Ganganaw Lornya
turned into the evening star."
Burun Burun the kingfisher
was sad because he lost his dog.

I enjoyed everything; but the year was coming when I was turning between six and seven. Mr Love talked to my parents about me living in the hostel. We called it a dormitory.

They were a bit sad losing me. I had two brothers but they both died. And a brother and sister from another mother. In those early days my father had three wives, one from each tribe.

RAIN

I am the one who made man
with my bare hands and with my sweat
I will own the land!

One was Ngarinyin, another was Wunambal and the other was Worrora. Those two brothers were from the Wunambal lady. When they both died I was the only one left.

After a long time my father became a Christian and Mr Love told him to have only one wife. It was a sad thing to do in tribal ways. Yes, the separation time came and he did give away his two wives.

BIND WITH THE WHITE MAN'S LAW

Oh Mother Land you are crying out,
"Come back, why have you left me alone?
The white man's law still binds you.
The time will come when you must pass -
I am lost without you, thinking of the times,
the days when you were here,
so proud in your Mother Land,
full of birds singing, a nature place.
You heard frogs croaking near the pool.
You should enjoy everything."

Yes, goodbye Mother Land -
I am bind with the white man's law.

He wanted to keep the Wunambal lady, so he gave my mother away to another old man. I called him uncle. I thought it was a joke, giving away his wives. I still stayed with my father, at the mission.

The day was coming for me to leave and stay with the other girls in the hostel. First of all I didn't want to go. I thought I was stepping to another world, "I have to go to school and learn the white man's ways."

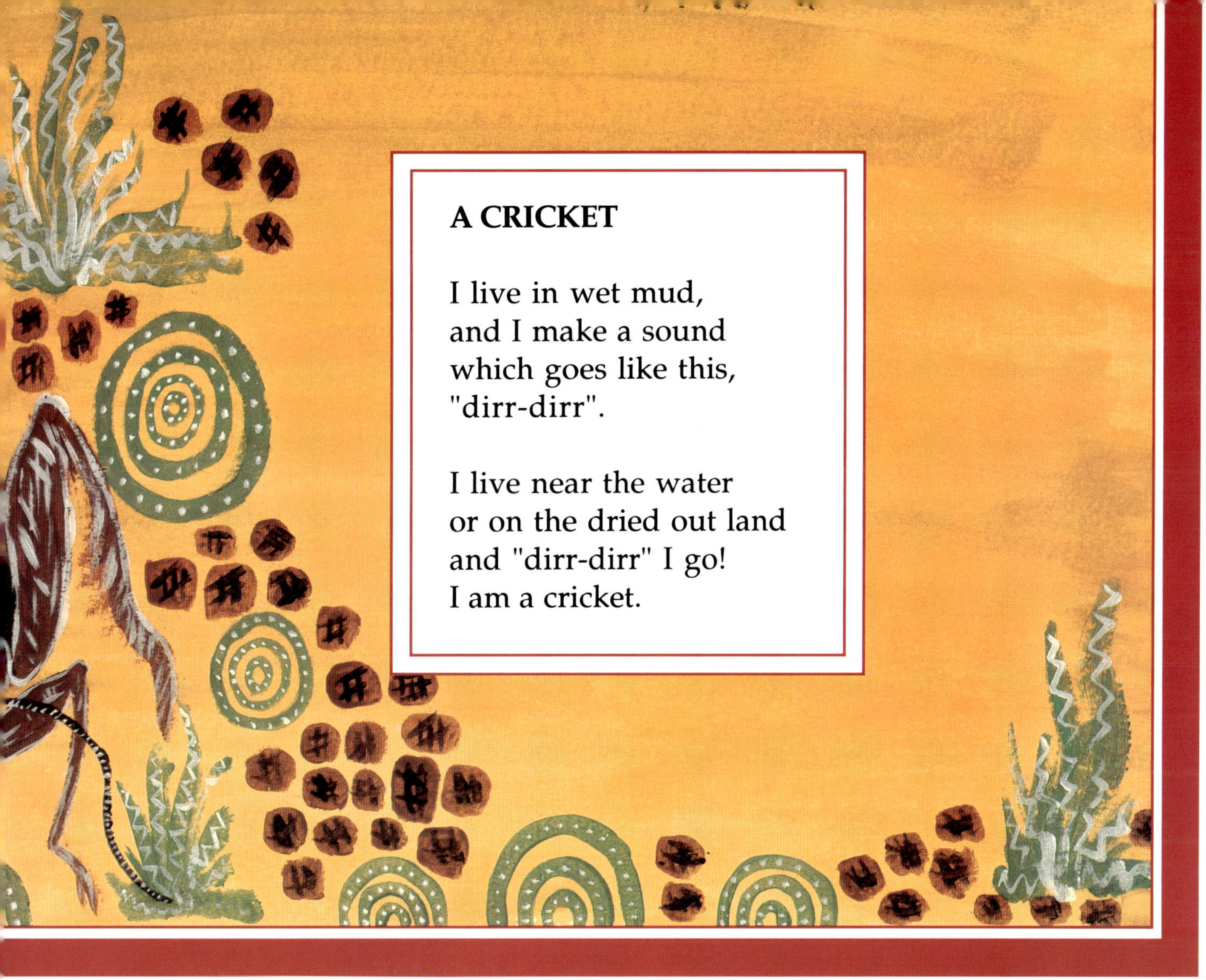

A CRICKET

I live in wet mud,
and I make a sound
which goes like this,
"dirr-dirr".

I live near the water
or on the dried out land
and "dirr-dirr" I go!
I am a cricket.

I missed all the things which my grandmother and my mother taught me, but I had a chance on school holidays. I went out bush, camping out for three weeks or so. I had a grand time with my parents again.

One person I missed was my mother. She went to a station with my uncle. Only at Christmas time she came to visit me. And then she got two children, a boy and a girl, which made her happy; she missed me a lot.

MOTHER'S TOUCH

Oh Mother once you taught me
by touching my eyes with your warm hands
and repeating, "Do not see evil things."
And again you warmed your hands
and touched my nose repeating,
"Do not sniff around and beg for food."
And again, mother dear, you warmed your hands
and touched my mouth repeating,
saying, "Do not use bad languages."
Oh, Mother all is well!

When I went out bush my father and my grandparents showed me the cave of the Wandjina, the spirit. And I asked many questions about this Wandjina, of my old people.

WANDJINAS

These are the three that taught us the rules
and with that they gave us land.
Each tribe its own country,
that's why the three are remembered
from the Dreamtime until today,

NGARMARALI   WANDALIE   WANARBRI

This is what they told me: the Wandjina is our God, he's the one which gave us everything, the land, our country, our dreamtime stories, that's what my parents told me.

I believed the way they told me dreamtime stories; but the one in church, Mr Love, taught me about God, saying "He is the Wandjina!" My mind was swirling around. Which God should I believe, the one in the caves or the one in the sky?

My father Pompey and my mother told me when I was older that my real father was killed in a tribal war.

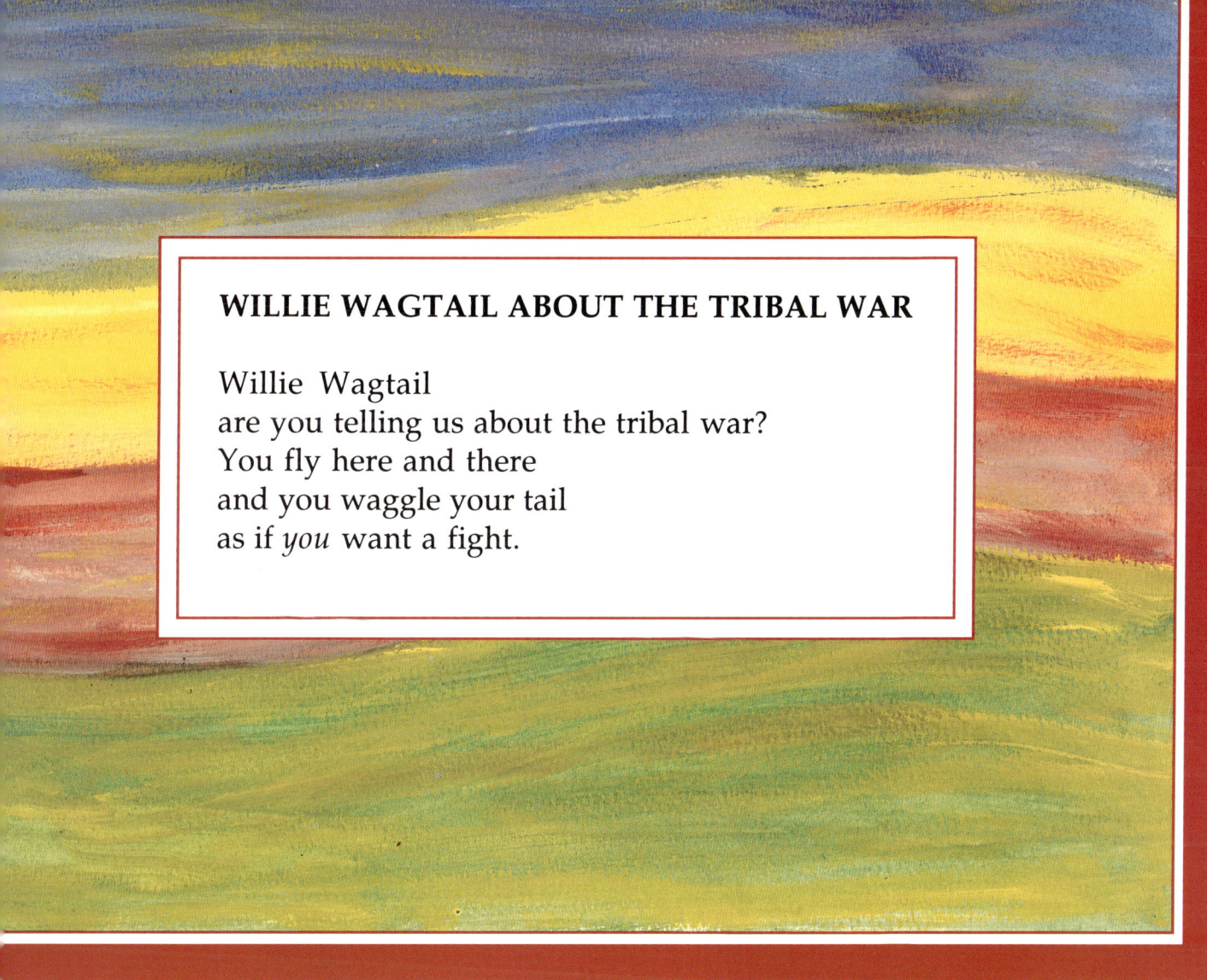

WILLIE WAGTAIL ABOUT THE TRIBAL WAR

Willie Wagtail
are you telling us about the tribal war?
You fly here and there
and you waggle your tail
as if *you* want a fight.

Pompey was my father's brother; he took my mother, when my father was dead and that's why he had three wives.

I learned to read and write at Kunmunya. Mrs McDougall was my teacher. The school had about twelve children attending. School day lasted from eight o'clock until lunch time. After lunch, apart from work in the garden, we also were taught how to cook and do other domestic tasks.

POET

Where the black man hunted
in the heart of the bush he knew -
every water hole of his country -
when the sun was setting,
and his hunting was over, he slept
for the night beside the fire.

He lay thinking of another day
so proud he was - when he woke up
in the morning he could hear birds laughing
and see the trees waving in a thin cool air,
twisting their branches to and fro
as if they were saying, "Come come
I am your relative standing here."

Same with the rocks, the hills, the mountains
and the wind rushing by in a hot, dusty day
the black man still hunted -
and found his meat.

Then the time came for me to leave school; I was sad, but at least I was still staying in the dormitory. I did some domestic work in the company of some of the elderly women, in one of the mission houses.

When I was young I went out with my parents along the coast - I used to sit and look around at the beautiful things, insects, birds, animals, trees, clouds, mountains and river. I always thought, if only I could write about these things and the dreamtime stories!

CAT

I am the native cat, I dance everywhere.
I hop skip and jump, I jump on the flat stone
and dance and wobble my bum and hold my hips
and then I dance again.

I jump onto the rock and shake my legs
and again I jump to the ground
and walk with my bum in the air
and then I run into my cave.

So I used to make stories in my mind, and later on when we were shifted from Kunmunya to live in Derby, I was asked if I could write stories. I was very happy, and so I started writing.

When I was young in Kunmunya with the other girls, I was a Girl Guide and others were Brownies. We had Girls' Scouts too and when I came to Derby I was Assistant Cub Mistress.

A DOG'S TALE

Once in a Dreamtime the dogs had a meeting:
"But before we sit down on the ground
we must pull our tails off!" So they did
and put them on the log...

When the enemy arrived they all rushed out
and forgot about their tails.
Three or two remembered and gave a shout
"Our tails!" - and they all ran back and put their tails on.

But it was one another's tails they put on!

I was happy doing that but leaving my tribal land I often think how nice it would be to go back up there. Mowanjum is our home now. The name Mowanjum means settled at last. But I left my traditional country.

I always dream of the life my people used to lead before the Europeans came. Here I am a linguist, helping Joyce Hudson, Therese Carr and Bill McGregor.

BLACK MAN

I am thinking of the mountains,
memories tumbling out of my head
Now all is gone.
What must I do?
Good times and bad I spend in civilization.
Will I go back to my hills and mountains
and hear the whistle of the curlews all night long,
echoes of the rushing stream,
the wind rustling by and the owls calling.
The frog croaks and sleeps,
I long to see the stars smile down
at me!

Up in Kunmunya I was a teacher, and also in Derby a kindergarten teacher and here I am still doing things, going about telling stories to schools.

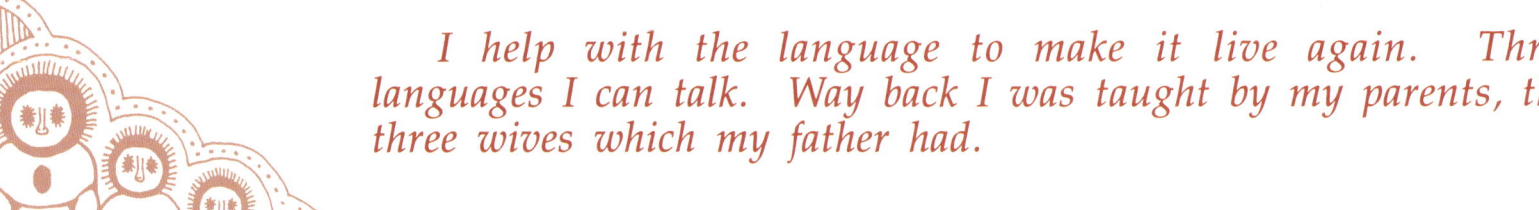

I help with the language to make it live again. Three languages I can talk. Way back I was taught by my parents, the three wives which my father had.

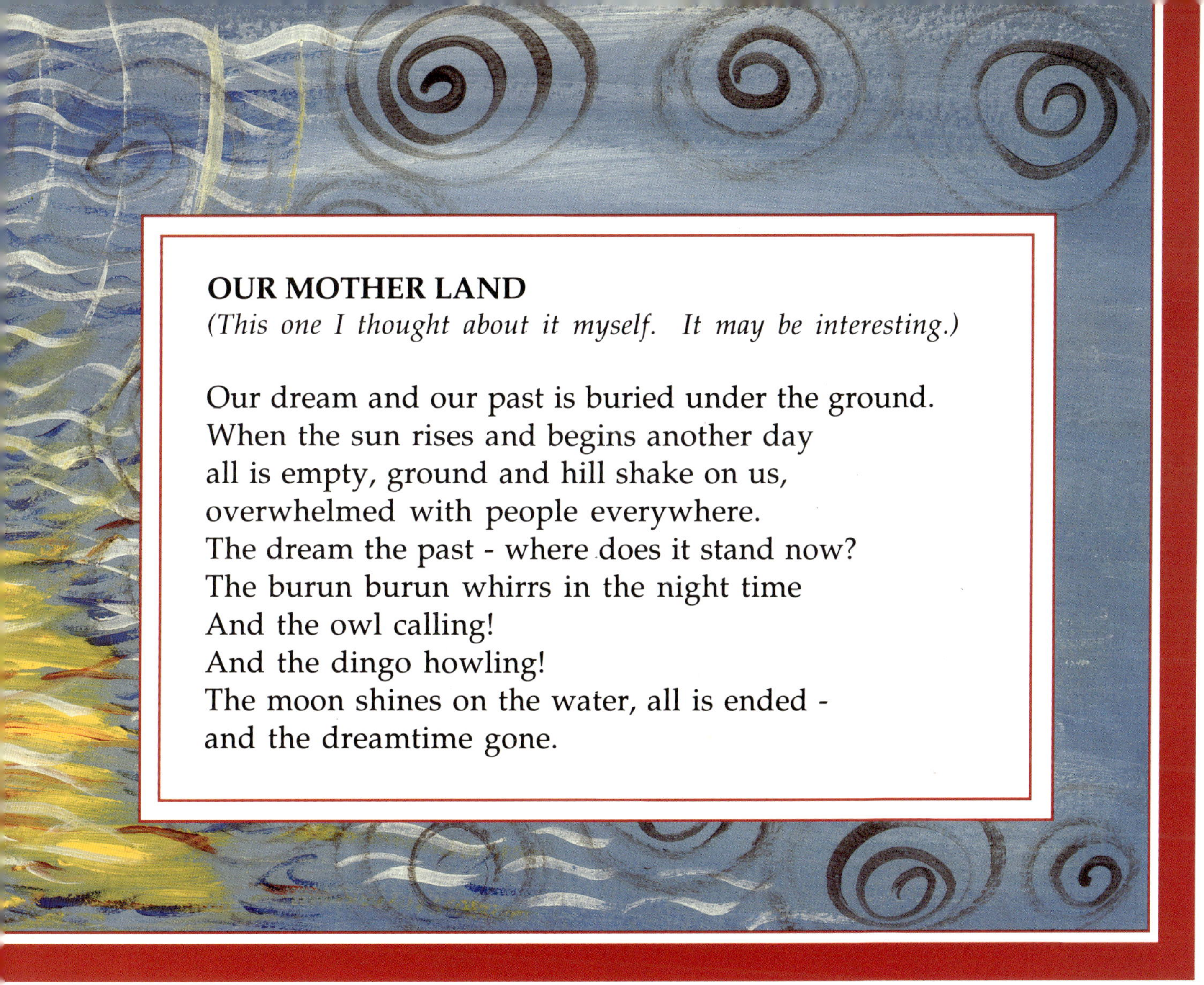

OUR MOTHER LAND

(This one I thought about it myself. It may be interesting.)

Our dream and our past is buried under the ground.
When the sun rises and begins another day
all is empty, ground and hill shake on us,
overwhelmed with people everywhere.
The dream the past - where does it stand now?
The burun burun whirrs in the night time
And the owl calling!
And the dingo howling!
The moon shines on the water, all is ended -
and the dreamtime gone.

One was Ngarinyin, that's my mother, one was Wunambal, that's my two brothers' mother, and one was Worrora. That's why I learned to talk the three and that is how I lived as I grew up. And now I am getting old.